Artie is Awesome

ARTIE'S ADVENTURES

DEIDRA DARST

To my son, Colin:
You are awesome. Always be proud of who you are.

To my son, Finley:
You are an amazing big brother. Never change.

Every child is special, I tell you that's true –
Your eyes, your smile, all specially you.

No two are alike, all are unique!
No one's like you, wherever you seek.

Every person in the world is different, you see –
Their own talents, soul, and personality.

How different we are, "thank goodness!" We exclaim –
How dull it would be if we were all just the same.

If everyone acted just like you,
We might as well be robots and look alike too!

How silly that would be, a class full of robots!
(in your best robot voice...)
"Hello.
How are you?
My name is Snore-a-lots."

How boring that would be, "Snore-a-lots" is right,
That's why we're all different, to make this world bright!

Each person you meet has their own little shimmer,
They stand out in a crowd, oh look how they glimmer!

We are all our own person, not like another,
So dare to be different, don't copy your brother.

Some kids like to read, some like to hike—
Some love to make messes, some ride a bike.

Some always act nicely and are very polite....
Others eat boogers and toot through the night!

Now that we know that "different" is cool —
I want to introduce you to a new kid at school.

His name is Artie, he's funny and sweet.
He loves his toy trains and pizza to eat.

You might notice that he doesn't look at your eyes,
He might get upset...and sometimes he cries.

He flaps his hands and has some different mannerisms —
That's because he has autism.

Artie loves order and wants things to stay the same,

And he might get upset when his routine has to change.

He doesn't always understand things that you say,
And he has been known to run away.

His autism can make some things a bit hard –
Like talking, and playing, and staying calm in the
yard.

We notice that Artie learns a bit differently,
So more help he needs, and we give it gently.

Artie is different, but he isn't broken –
He "talks" with a device, just listen! He's
outspoken.

Artie loves to play, he might line up blocks.
He also loves numbers and stares at the clocks.

Artie is fast and he loves to run –
When you play tag, ask him to join in your fun.

The things that are easy for you and for me –
Well they're hard for Artie, just watch and you'll
see.

Kids like Artie work so hard to get where they
are–
We could all learn a lesson, because they set a
high bar.

Autism is different, I've explained in our chat—
But it doesn't mean "bad," I hope you know that!

They're still smart and funny, and have feelings too,
So please be their friend, the truest of true.

Try to include your new friend Artie –
You'll learn that he's fun, maybe the life of the party!

If your class takes a trip, and you go to the zoo–
You might laugh together when that monkey throws poo!

We celebrate our differences, we just aren't the same.

(Because remember those robots? They were sooooo lame.)

We all have special qualities that we didn't pick:
Some are creative and some are autistic.

Always remember to be your best you,
And our friends like Artie will do the same too.

I'm glad that we're different, it keeps things exciting.
Now always remember to be nice and inviting.

The
End

Deidra Darst is available for speaking engagements. Inquiries can be made on

www.theSLPmom.com

Made in the USA
Middletown, DE
05 December 2020